Tate Olszewski Books.

Proudly Presents:

Virtuous Kingdoms.

Written In 2020.

By: Tate Olszewski.

Running off startled into the distance after suddenly striking

the books out of her hands that she carry while strolling

along the pathway into the the wet muddy surface of the

soil, were the young group of youthful boys upon noticing

the young boy in the distance as he silently approached…

Chapter One: Along The Pathway!

Picking up the now soggy books water dripping from their

pages & handing her the still dry books that he himself

carried along the pathway that morning, keeping her now

ruined books for himself proceeding together along the trail

silently until reaching the academy parting ways for their

daily schedule of academic studies physical trainings...

Walking into the study area directly towards the group of

young men who had early slapped the stack of books from

her hand, setting the ruined books onto the table's surface

beside them splashing mud from their water-soaked pages

onto the academic uniforms that they proudly each wear!

"One day I will be in the chambers! What you did to her was

mean and wrong! You owe her an apology! You shall cause

her family and friends no more problems in the future! By

the end of this academic day you will all formally apologize!

Each of you will give her one of your books until she has all of

her books back! If not I will ensure she receives them from

you all myself personally while sending her your apologies

indirectly if need be, but I warn you if that be the case that

our future presents us with this as our fates, than we warned

I shall personally take those books from you and return to

her every book that you caused her to lose on the path in the

rain this morning earlier this day!"

"Alright! But you and I both know her family's kind doesn't

belong in our land! We will each return one book to her of

our own until she has received all of her books back dry, but

just know that you can not promote their ways in our lands

forever! One day our lands will conquer her homelands!"

"You are wrong! You will apologize to her by end of the day

today, and you will give her your books until she has hers

fully returned to her, we can address this with her teacher?"

"That is enough everybody! Please focus your attention on

today's academics! Kingdom trade routes! We can not

sustain our current kingdom growth rates by simply confining

our markets to our own specific lands! Our current systems

require the expansion into vast new frontiers of distant

lands! Encountering many cultures along our way benefiting

both kingdoms and beyond greatly! But unfortunately since

you all have arrived here late we are out of time for today…

Go on your way pondering the words that I have said!"

"Hey it's the girl from earlier! She must also be on her way

returning home for the day… We are sorry about earlier in

the rain! We shouldn't have done that! Here are some books

from each of us to replace your damaged books! We won't

trouble you it your family and friends again…"

"Apology accepted. There isn't need for you to cause us

hardships in our being here in this land we are good people!"

"We should get out of here… Look who is coming around the

corner of the path!"

Running up throwing her arms around him in a thankful

hugging embrace the group of bullies cowardly sneak away in

the moment as he looking into her eyes gently begins saying

"Those guys don't really truly want to mess with me, one day

I will speak in the chambers and the whole kingdom and all of

its lands will hear what I say! I am sorry that people from my

lands would purposely do something like that to you, but

hugging me isn't necessary… What they did to you was

wrong and they will not bother you again in the future!"

"Surely those goons would have never returned proper

books to me without what ever it is you did to intervene after

while I attended academics! I owe you a thank you of some

kind!"

"No, you don't! You owe me nothing! They shouldn't have

done what they did! They fear your countries greatly vast

culture and wealth overtaking that of their own, that's all…"

"They need not fear us, for it is there own creation of

improper governing systems that will lead to their collapse

and demise! Not our peaceful culture promoting prosperity

for all! My homelands were once bountiful and flourishing

beyond all expectations until these new trade negotiate

forced our family into exile here in these strange new lands!"

"I didn't know, I am sorry your family is experiencing all this!"

"It is not your fault, however if they move further with these new trade regulation agreements both our lands may be in trouble in the future! Not just that of my home-lands! But for yours and many other as well, all who encounter the trades!"

<u>Chapter Two: Within The Chambers!</u>

Within the walls of the great chambers that very day while

the kids attended scheduled daily academics studying,

learning, and playing, the stern voices of council members

could be heard saying "In the hall of this great chamber

please hear my words! This new trade regulation agreement

deceptively threatens us all! This nearing invasion of my

homelands be-fronts many more to all of your lands as well

to every foreign shore! They have established a system

ridden with greed, not that of the betterment of all! True

wealth and prosperity for everybody! They will use the initial

invasion of my homelands to establish a foothold to launch

future attacks against you all as they have done to many

decimating all who oppose their trade system designed to captive all it encounters, enforced through brutal horrific military attacks and constraining restraints! If we all do not stand together in this defining moment our fates may eternally be sealed unto dire circumstances from which we all may not recover fully at cost of our once bountiful lands! Do not allow them to use invading our lands, to attack you!"

"Great grand Chamber I interrupt so abruptly to inform you" that our loyal forces have advanced our trade empire further than its borders have ever been into vast new territories that surely hold vast wealth's in raw resources that are ours for the taking! We offer trade fairly, but for those who refuse assimilation is our only option! As we can not afford these resources to be kept in hands of our openly declared enemies! We must push forward our expansion! Our trade system depends on it and we can not allow it to fail! Do not

listen nor side with him for it will assuredly only bring

hardship and decimation to your homelands as well, like his!"

"Hear my pleas! I do not approach you seeking own wealth

but to offer salvation from that which endangering us all!"

"The council can not and must not allow these foreigners to

disrupt our established trade systems or we shall all suffer!

We must confiscate those resources to sustain our growth!"

Breaking the tension of that moment a voice decrees in a

stern and harsh tone... "The council will vote and decide as to

whether or not intervene in the proceeding forward of the

gadaffen invasion and take over! Any in favour, say I?"

All except two nation's chamber members erupting with I's,

the fates of so many lives were soon to be uprooted solely

benefiting a very few minority among the vast populations!

The invasions proceeding to decimate all of those in

opposition to the enslaving and newly captive ways! Though

the use of brutally horrific military force this would be

enforced, and mandatorily regulated so that none could

escape the reaches of its direly hazardous systems in place!

Chapter Three: Life Moves Forward!

As the years pass the academic studies as well as careers

advanced, when entering the door to a distant restaurant

eatery he notices a girl that he recognizes from his past! In

that moment his joy fading suddenly as he sees the group of

men she served as they jerkily harassed the exotic foreign

beauty that once had walked a remembered muddy path...

"Hey! You all really shouldn't trouble her! Years ago I told you all this as youths in the academy! I walk in here today and happen to see you up to the same old things? You all should be ashamed! Leave until you can properly behave!"

"Now that's no way to speak to the newest chamber member!"

"You nor I are chamber members yet! Your family better represent the people properly, for not just their interests but your as well it is your futures interests best bet! No leave her alone or you will further be disrespecting our lands throne!"

"Please there is no need to quarrel over my wellness! It is both of your first time in my new establishment peacefully I welcome you both, just don't you quarrel amongst anyone!"

"Agreed! Peacefulness is always best, I apologize my lady!"

"That's ok we were just troublesomely leaving! One day I will

see you in the chambers as I receive the councils approvals!"

"Leave now & reconsider your ways before it leads to your

disgrace, and downfall in the records of our history books!"

Chapter Four: Meanwhile In The Chambers!

"Just as spoken in the past these horrific realities have come

to pass! As Gadaffen lands once were invaded shortly upon

his very pleas within this chamber went unheard! A true

sharing of the wealth, not just elitism! Now before you here I

stand the free leader of a truly great lands, with vastly

ancient cultures and disappearing wealth's beyond the

dreams of man! As told before invaders occupy our lands!

Utilizing occupied launch points to wage their attacks!

Unheard were warnings before... What will come of the

future for our lands? They will continue to murder, killing as

they invade every foreign land! Their systems of trade

require it! You have deceitfully entered into tyranny against

your lands! The theft of all known resources! For the

enslavement of your lands! Corrupt systems will be your

downfall and it does not have to be thus way! We could all

stand united to accomplish things that will be remembered

throughout history not just as right today but something truly

great for all to know as their inspiring heritage honouring

those who on this day instead of greed chose what is right for

every bodies future and our historic legacy! Here my similar

pleas in these chambers today! Do not turn your backs and

simply look away for as forewarned this very situation will

affect your nations in day! Prosperity for all does not have to

come byway of the impoverishing life of those you enslaved!

Trust my words hear my pleas Save us all both you and me!”
My lands are known Sumeran please help lands remain free!”

“We have Successfully destroyed all minor forces standing I

our expansions way this is the last meeting in the chamber

prior to the new academic graduates taking control! It is our

last chance to ensure our trade systems push forward!”

Chapter Five: New To The Chambers!

Upon venturing forth along his way stopping pond-side by a

small lake to allow his horse and men to rest, a graceful

figure emerges from the distant horizon traveling fast as her

stallion full gallop arrives placing both front hooves kicking

into the air! Mounted on its back saddled on its back an

exotic familiar figure confidently elegantly set saying

assuredly directly right to him startling him as he bathed!

"You never have told me your name?"

Responding naked in the waters without any of clothes on…

"My name is not important, this quest isn't about fame! It is

meant with greater purpose, even in those academic days!"

Dismounting her stead her voice breaking the silence of the

moment "I once told you in our past that these new trade

regulations affect the peoples of my lands too! My words

were honest, I spoke the truth! Still even here now today!

Honest I remain, in hopes of your spoken truths being heard

in the chambers spearheading not body but peaceful truths!

Will you do this? Will you speak to those in the chamber? Tell

them our lands are great and our culture beyond ancient, we

wish all for peace, and freedom and prosperity to all not

violent captivity and enforced militaristic slavery of corrupted

systems governing various kingdoms access to sustainable

trade with others!"

"Yes upon my being sworn in I will most certainly address

that of which issues you speak! You know me, I believe in

your dream! I'm still that same small boy from the academy!"

Chapter Six: Chambers Once More:

Mounting her stallion quite happily satisfied with her early

morning encounter, hooves begin trotting as she looks

forward into the horizon galloping full speed away!

Later that in the night after an uneventful few days journey

arriving to the grand hall of the chambers that had

determined the pathway fate of the kingdoms lands

throughout its history, entering the grand doorway not

splendorous but purposefully addressing its members

without hesitation! "We are gathered here today to honor a

rightful tradition of transition! Eject me as you may, but let it

be forever on records spoken! There is no need for imposing

our self enslaving systems of trade on any other nation! No

kingdom should ever bear military actions against them for

simply trying to ensure the wealth and prosperity of that

beyond their own nations but including every living soul in

our existence! We in this transitional period can choose a

better path forward girl ourselves and future generations to

come! In these very chambers on days truly great voices

were once ignored allowing direness to become rampant! I

plea do not make the same continued mistake into our future! Many generations to come… All generations yo come in the future bear the consequences of choices in this chamber today! Let us be remembered throughout history as those who transition our legacy into something truly great!"

"Guards seize him! His treacherous tongue defiles this great chamber!" Suddenly interrupting the inspirational speech, can be heard by all as its echo still screeched! I too am one of those transitioning few, new to take control and I assure you all that our systems will remain in place! Expanding globally!"

Chapter Seven: Foreign Diplomacy!

Crashing through the grand doors in that moment almost

flying with hooves in the air, was an exotic foreign beauty

mounted on her stallion! Elegant and graceful as they all

shockingly stared her beauty stunning with her flowing the

breeze long dark hair! Her eyes piercing gaze stunning the

room… "This chamber was once sacred! Honorable indeed!

But it like your empire has succumb to greedy thieves! No

more shall you squander the resources if nations wealth for

your own, just to later enslave them in a tree system not

natural to their lands but only to that of your own! In my

hand is a letter signed from every major king! I'd every major

land this is the message that it reads… We have conversed

and mutually agree that their needs to end all war and we

need to ensure future peace, not just that but always nit to

just some elitist few but prosperity for all even those nit in

this chambers room! Listen to her words! For the sake of a

better world not just for the chamber, but for the better of

us all! Our futures will be brighter! Mire prosperous for all,

not just for those in this grand hall! Thank you, everyone!"

"Guards seize this traitor who's letter belongs in the mud the same as I placed her books in the mud long ago! Stop them!"

"You guards shall do no such thing! I have known this gracefully elegant stallion mounted woman ever since I was a child! In being a chamber member I say we do it the honest truthful democratic way! Every leader & kingdom's nation has all united in agreement to ensure peace, and prosperity for all! Together we all stand united! So shall we remain into the that of our futures! Let it be known throughout all of history to come, that here on this day we did what is right!"

The End!